BILL CLINTON

President of the 90s

by Robert Cwiklik

The Millbrook Press
Brookfield, Connecticut
A Gateway Biography

Cover photograph courtesy of Paul S. Howell/Gamma Liaison

Photographs courtesy of Corbis-Bettmann: pp. 4, 21; Gamma
Liaison: pp. 7 (both), 10 (bottom), 18, 28 (© Cynthia Johnson),
39 (top: © Brad Markel, bottom: © Porter Gifford), 43 (©
Cynthia Johnson); Sygma: p. 10 (top), 15, 24; © Robert Kusel/
Tony Stone Images: p. 41.

Library of Congress Cataloging-in-Publication Data
Cwiklik, Robert.
Bill Clinton : president of the 90s / by Robert Cwiklik.
   p.   cm. — (A Gateway biography)
Includes bibliographical references and index.
Summary: Chronicles the life of Bill Clinton from his childhood
in Arkansas to his governorship of that state and his first term as
president of the United States, including highlights from the
1996 presidential campaign.
ISBN 0-7613-0129-1 (lib. bdg.) 0-7613-0146-1 (pbk.)
1. Clinton, Bill, 1946–   —Juvenile literature. 2. Presidents—
United States—Biography—Juvenile literature. I. Title.
II. Series.
E886.C87   1997
973.929'092—dc21   [B]   97-797   CIP   AC

Published by The Millbrook Press, Inc.
2 Old New Milford Road
Brookfield, Connecticut 06804

BILL CLINTON

Bill Clinton, the Democrats' nominee for president, prepares to give his acceptance speech at their convention in New York City in 1992.

On *Thursday, July 16, 1992,* Bill Clinton, governor of Arkansas, walked onto the stage at Madison Square Garden in New York City. The arena was packed with thousands of people for the national convention of the Democratic party. All eyes were on Clinton as he stepped up to accept the nomination of his party for the presidency of the United States.

Millions would see Clinton's speech on television. In November he would run against President George Bush to see which man voters would elect as their president for the next four years.

Clinton, a handsome forty-five-year-old, was much younger than the president, although his bushy brown hair had gone mostly gray. In his speech, he asked Americans to choose a "new generation" of leaders. He promised to fight for the "forgotten" people, those "who do the work, pay the taxes, raise the kids and play by the rules."

Voters seemed to like Clinton's call to the "forgotten middle class." After the convention, he surged ahead of Bush in the polls. But there were still months to go before the election, and Americans did not often vote out sitting presidents. Clinton braced for the fight of his life.

Bill Clinton's father, William Jefferson Blythe III, a car salesman, and his mother, Virginia Cassidy, a nurse, were married in 1941 in Shreveport, Louisiana. Blythe was in the service during World War II. When he came home, the best job he could find was in far-off Chicago. Virginia stayed behind, and when she found she was pregnant moved in with her parents in the small town of Hope, Arkansas. Blythe made the long drive there to see his family whenever he could. But one tragic night, his car crashed into a ditch and he was killed. Three months later, on August 19, 1946, Virginia gave birth to a son. She named him William Jefferson Blythe IV, after the father he would never meet.

Virginia needed training for a better-paying job, so she would be able to support herself and her baby. She left little "Billy" with her parents while she studied in New Orleans to become a nurse-anesthetist. Bill's grandparents were not well educated, but they saw the value of learning and disci-

*Bill at eighteen
months, and . . .*

*. . . as a four-year-old
Arkansas cowboy.*

pline. They taught Bill to count and to read. When he was in first grade, he was already reading the newspaper.

In 1950, Virginia married Roger Clinton, a car salesman. When Bill was seven, the family moved to Hot Springs, Arkansas. The boy was known as Bill Clinton by classmates, although he did not legally change his name until he was a teenager. He was an excellent student, always eager to learn. Sometimes teachers found him too eager. He once got a D in conduct because, his teacher said, he always knew the answers in class and did not give others a chance to speak.

But while Bill's future as a student was bright, there were dark days at home. Roger Clinton drank heavily and had a hot temper. When he was drunk he sometimes hit his wife and the child they had together, Roger, Jr., born when Bill was ten. During one tantrum, he fired a gun in the house. One day, when Bill was fourteen years old, his patience ran out. Roger senior was drunk and bullying Virginia and Roger, Jr. Bill stepped into his path. "You'll never hit either of them again," he said sternly. "If you want them, you'll have to go through me." Roger Clinton's violence against his family stopped.

*T*he adults around Bill noticed early on that he was a natural leader among his classmates. He was elected president of his junior class in high school. At seventeen, he attended Boys State, a camp where students learned about politics. Bill was elected a delegate to Boys Nation, a gathering of teenagers from around the country in Washington, D.C. The group visited the White House, where Bill shook hands with his hero, President John F. Kennedy. That handshake changed Bill Clinton's life. After meeting Kennedy, he knew, as his mother put it, that "politics was the answer for him."

Music was also a big part of Bill's life. He played the saxophone in a three-piece jazz band called Three Blind Mice. He was also a leader in the high school band. But he still found time to excel in his studies. He became a National Merit Scholarship semifinalist and graduated fourth in his class of 323. Carolyn Staley, a friend from high school, said that in everything Bill did, "he had to be the best."

*Bill met his
hero, President
John F. Kennedy,
on a trip to the
White House with
the Boys Nation
youth group.*

*A triumphant-looking
Bill on his high school
graduation day.*

Bill was offered a scholarship to study music in college. Instead, he went to Georgetown University, in Washington, D.C., to study international affairs. There he began to prepare for a life in politics.

At Georgetown, Bill Clinton met students and teachers "from all over the country and all over the world." It was, he said, "like a feast."

But Clinton had to take part-time jobs to help pay for his costly education. One summer, he went back to Arkansas and worked for Frank Holt, who was running for governor. Holt lost, but his nephew, an Arkansas Supreme Court justice, helped Clinton get a job in the Washington office of Arkansas Senator J. William Fulbright.

Clinton stayed as active as ever in school. He was elected president of both his freshman and sophomore classes at Georgetown. He impressed fellow students as a focused, hardworking man. Everyone could see, as one classmate later said, that he was "very political." Clinton was such a fine student that some of his professors told him to apply for a Rhodes scholarship. Each year, Oxford University in England gives top college students the chance to study there after they graduate. Clinton didn't think he would ever be selected. When he was, he called his mother and asked, "How do you think I'll look in English tweed?"

In 1968, Clinton graduated from Georgetown and headed off for Oxford. Since his scholarship paid his way, he didn't have to work and could give all his time to his studies. The rich fund of knowledge and culture at Oxford thrilled him. He read more widely than ever, finding many new interests. "I read about three hundred books both years I was there," he said. A friend from those days said that Clinton was "interested in everything."

A crisis was brewing in the United States while Clinton was at Oxford. America was fighting a war in Vietnam. Officials said the war had to be won to stop Communists from taking over all of Southeast Asia. But many people opposed the war. Some said it was wrong to fight because Vietnam was no threat to our security.

Some young men refused to serve in the military when they were drafted, which was a crime. Others looked for legal ways to avoid service.

Clinton had a student deferment—permission not to serve until he finished his studies. He strongly believed the war was wrong and even helped organize protests against it while in England. When his deferment ran out, he took his chances in the draft lottery. In this system, young men's birthdates were drawn by lot. Only those born on the earliest dates picked were drafted. Clinton's birthdate was one of the last picked, so he was not drafted. His escape from service seemed honorable. But details of it would come back to haunt him.

Although Clinton was happy at Oxford, he chose to leave after two years. He left to take a scholarship at Yale Law School. Getting a law degree was a big part of his long-term plan to enter politics. Many of Clinton's professors at Yale had served in the government under John F. Kennedy. That sort of legal work—public service—was exactly what Clinton had in mind.

One of Clinton's classmates at Yale was a smart, pretty young woman whom he found himself staring at in class. He was afraid to talk to her. But one day, she walked up to him and spoke. "Look," she said, "if you're going to keep staring at me, and I'm going to keep staring back, I think we should at least know each other. I'm Hillary Rodham."

Clinton would soon call Hillary "the smartest person I've ever known." Before long, they were a couple. In 1972, they both took time off from Yale to work on the presidential campaign of George McGovern. Although McGovern lost the election to Richard Nixon, the campaign taught the young law students a lot about big-time politics.

Graduates of Yale Law School were always in demand. After Bill and Hillary graduated, both were offered good jobs in Washington. They were asked to work on the staff of the House Judiciary Committee. It was looking into the possible criminal involvement of President Richard Nixon and his aides in what was known as the Watergate scandal. Most new lawyers would have jumped at the chance to work there. Rodham took the job. But as for Clinton, his next stop was Arkansas.

Back in 1967, when twenty-one-year-old Bill Clinton was still a student at Georgetown, Roger Clinton was dying of cancer. Bill often made the

Bill met his future wife, Hillary, at Yale Law School.

long drive from Washington to visit him. He wanted to make peace with his stepfather before the end came. "I think he knew that I was coming down there just because I loved him," he later said.

After six weeks, Roger Clinton died. Bill had lost another father. He had never really gotten over the loss of William Blythe, who died at the age of only twenty-nine. That tragedy made young Bill think about when he himself might die, something most children never do. It was one reason he always seemed in such a hurry. "I thought I had to live for myself and for him too," he said.

When Clinton got back to Arkansas, it might have seemed he was slowing down. He was happy to be in Arkansas, one of the poorest states in the country. He told his mother that he planned to "break his back" helping his state to prosper, if the people would let him.

Clinton learned that a teaching job was open in the Law School of the University of Arkansas at Fayetteville. But the dean said he was too young for the job. "I've been too young to do everything I've ever done," Clinton said. He was granted an interview—and got the job.

Fayetteville is a little college town tucked into the Ozark Mountains. It was a perfect place for a professor to settle down and enjoy the quiet life of the mind. But Clinton wanted action. Early in 1974, after teaching for only three months, he signed up to run for a seat in Congress. It was held by Republican John Hammerschmidt, who had served eight years and was very popular. Hardly anyone knew who Bill Clinton was.

That would soon change. Clinton ran a dogged campaign. He drove all around in his little car, jumping out to speak to groups of voters wherever he found them. Some politicians found such campaigning very tiring. Clinton loved it. He didn't expect to win. But he saw the campaign as "an experiment"— a way to learn politics by doing.

Clinton's experiment was a big success. He almost beat Hammerschmidt, who won with only 51.5 percent of the vote. People were stunned. A reporter called Clinton the "boy wonder" of Arkansas politics.

During the campaign, Hillary had left Washington to take a job at the University of Arkansas Law School at Fayetteville. Soon she was managing

Clinton's Fayetteville home during his 1974 campaign for Congress. He lost, but not by much. People began to know his name.

Clinton's campaign. But she was not sure she wanted to stay in Arkansas. One day, in 1975, while she and Clinton were out for a walk, they strolled by a cozy little house. Hillary said, in passing, that she liked it. Soon, when Hillary was out of town, Clinton went out and bought it. When he sprang his surprise, Hillary was shocked. "So you're going to have to marry me," he said. Two months later, she did.

C*linton had impressed people* with his peppy, well-run campaign. Many saw big things in his future. He quickly proved them right. He won election to the post of Arkansas attorney general in 1976. He was so popular the Republicans didn't even put up a candidate to oppose him.

Clinton was praised for taking on tough issues. As his fame spread, many hoped he would seek higher office. He did not let them down. In 1978, he ran for governor and won easily. At thirty-two, Clinton was the youngest governor in the country. He promised to improve education and to bring higher-paying jobs to Arkansas. His goal was to make the state "the envy of the nation."

Clinton launched a sweeping reform plan. His main concern was education. Ever since he was a teenager, he had said that people in Arkansas were just as smart as people anywhere. If they didn't do well in national tests, it was because Arkansas spent less on schools and teachers than most other states. Clinton wanted to raise teachers' pay. But he also wanted new teachers to pass an exam to prove they knew enough to teach. And he wanted to merge the 382 districts of the clumsy school system into bigger units that would be easier to work with.

Clinton was praised for his energy and intelligence. Even then, some people talked about him as a future candidate for the vice presidency, or even the presidency. But before long, his programs bogged down. Lawmakers would not come up with the money to fully pay for the teachers' raises. People grew angry about merging their hometown school districts with those of other towns. And voters were furious when, to pay for new roads, Clinton raised the fees for car licenses.

Clinton was praised for some of his school reforms. But mostly he faced criticism in the press. His popularity fell. Still, when he ran for reelection

Bill Clinton was elected governor of Arkansas for the first time at the age of thirty-two.

in 1980 (Arkansas governors served two-year terms then) most people expected him to win. But he lost a close election to Republican Frank White.

C*linton had looked* like a young man with a bright future in politics. Now it all seemed swept away. His mood was dark. What had gone wrong? He concluded that the people thought he cared only about advancing his own political career. They thought he didn't care enough about them.

Clinton saw that he had tried to do too much, too soon. If he got another chance to serve, he promised to take time to explain his programs to the people and win their support.

Governor White was having problems of his own. He had no plan for running the state and was not on top of the issues. He once signed a bill without even reading it first. Some people called him "Governor Goofy."

Clinton was soon back in public view, making speeches critical of Governor White. In February 1982, he said he was running for governor again and that he'd learned from his mistakes. At campaign events, Clinton now asked people to tell him what was on their minds. "You can't lead without listening," he liked to say.

Governor White could not run away from his poor record. Clinton won the election. Voters gave him another chance. It was the first time in Arkansas history that a governor who had been beaten won office again.

Education reform was again the main item in Clinton's program. He asked for more money for schools, higher standards for students, and testing for all teachers, not just new ones.

Teachers said it was not fair to ask experienced teachers to risk their jobs if they failed a test. But Clinton did not back down. He had put Hillary at the head of a committee on educational standards. She helped explain his program to the people. With her help, Clinton convinced them the plan was sound. The legislature passed it into law.

By 1988, many people saw Bill Clinton as a man who might be president one day. He had won the Arkansas governorship again in 1986 (a change in

Clinton, reelected governor of Arkansas,
drives slowly through town in a parade with Hillary
and their two-year-old daughter, Chelsea.

the law gave him a four-year term). After that, all his actions were studied for clues to his plans. If he made a speech out of state, reporters said he was trying to build a national following. They expected him to run for president in 1988 and were surprised when he did not.

On July 20, 1988, at the Democratic convention in Atlanta, Bill Clinton gave the speech nominating Michael Dukakis for president. It was a wonderful chance to reach people all over the nation who were watching on television. But everything went wrong. The lights were never dimmed. No one in the hall seemed to be listening. His words were drowned out by chants of "We want Mike!" The speech seemed to last forever. When he finally said, "In conclusion," the hall exploded in cheers, as if the crowd was saying, "Thank God that's over."

Clinton became the butt of jokes. "What a windbag," said talk-show host Johnny Carson. But two nights later, Clinton went on Carson's show, cracked jokes about his speech, and even played a saxophone solo. The audience gave him a big round of applause. "Your saving grace is that you have a good sense of humor," Carson said.

In 1990, Clinton ran for reelection to a fifth term as governor. Voters wondered if he would desert Arkansas in the middle of his term to run for president. Clinton promised to "serve four years" if elected. He won easily again.

Meanwhile, Clinton was often in the national spotlight. In 1989, President Bush asked him to be co-chairman of a national meeting of governors to talk about ways to improve education in the United States. In 1990, he was named chairman of the Democratic Leadership Council (DLC), a group of mostly southern party leaders who said Democrats had to change their message to win the presidency.

In the 1980s, Democrats were seen as the party of high taxes and wasteful "big government." Ronald Reagan, a Republican, was elected president in 1980 and 1984, and his vice president, George Bush, was elected president in 1988, by promising lower taxes and "smaller government." But by 1991, Republicans were in trouble. Taxes had been cut, mostly for the rich, who were making more money than ever. But Democrats claimed that the rich did not invest their money to create jobs as much as Republicans said they would. Millions were without jobs. And since taxes were lower, the government took in less money and built up a mountain of debt—over four *trillion* dollars by 1991.

Americans were starting to fear that the nation was in trouble. Democrats thought that if they could shed their "tax and spend" image they could win back the presidency. But probably not in 1992. President Bush was thought to be very popular after leading the way, in 1991, to victory in the Persian Gulf War with Iraq.

Clinton's trips out of state and visits to talk shows fed rumors back home that he would soon run for president. "I'm not running for anything," he would say. But in July 1991, he admitted, for the first time, that he was thinking about running in 1992. That made many in Arkansas angry. After all, he had promised not to run. In September, Clinton toured the state, asking people what they thought. Most voters were willing to release him from his promise if he thought running for the presidency would be good for Arkansas and for the country.

On October 3, 1991, Bill Clinton spoke to a large crowd in front of the Old State House in Little Rock. He said that he was running for president

Clinton announces that he will run for president.

because the nation was in danger of losing the American Dream. "The country is headed in the wrong direction fast, slipping behind, losing our way," Clinton told the cheering crowd. He called for higher taxes on the rich and tax breaks for people who make investments that create jobs. As he sketched his plan to rebuild the nation, not all Little Rock cheered. One critic wrote that Clinton's broken promise showed that "his word is dirt."

In November Clinton started campaigning in New Hampshire, site of the first presidential primary. Many states held such primaries. In these, voters picked the person they wanted to become their party's choice to run for president. Then that person would run against the choice of the other party. Five candidates besides Clinton were on the Democratic ballot, and one, former Senator Paul Tsongas from Massachusetts, was the early favorite. Few voters this far north had ever heard of the governor of Arkansas.

Clinton did not win the primary, but he finished second. This was remarkable because during the months before this primary two major scandals involving him had been talked about in the news. The first involved a woman named Gennifer Flowers who claimed she had had an affair with Clinton. Clinton and his wife went on TV together and he denied the affair, and then admitted their marriage had not been perfect. He said the problems were in the past, and would make no other comments. Most of the press and most of the voters felt he had said enough. His campaign was still alive.

The second scandal involved a letter Clinton had written while he was a college student during the Vietnam War. Some people said the letter showed that Clinton had schemed to "dodge the draft" to avoid military service during the war. Again Clinton denied the charges and explained away the evidence. Both of these stories raised questions about Clinton's character. Either one could have ended his political life forever. But at nine o'clock on Primary Day in New Hampshire, Bill Clinton called a press conference and declared that "New Hampshire, tonight, has made Bill Clinton the Comeback Kid." Clinton's second-place "win" made headlines, and he got a big boost in the national opinion polls.

Clinton kept campaigning hard. He swept the southern primaries and won other big contests: Pennsylvania, New York, Michigan, and Illinois. By the time he won California in June, he had the Democratic nomination sewn up. But was he strong enough to beat President Bush, the Republican nominee, in November? Some said he only looked strong next to the weak Democrats he had beaten in the primaries.

Polls showed that the scandals had left doubts about Clinton in the minds of many voters. They did not trust him. But voters were not happy with Bush either. After the glow of the victory over Iraq faded, their thoughts turned homeward. The steady loss of American jobs and the growing mountain of debt made many fear for the future. Bush did not seem to have a plan to turn things around.

Then Ross Perot, a feisty Texas billionaire, stormed into the race. He went on television and said the nation was in crisis and government was ignoring it. He said that government should be run like a business. Perot had never held public office. But since he was very successful in business, millions thought he could fix the nation's problems. It looked as if this "third party" candidate could have an effect on the outcome of the election.

Meanwhile, Bill Clinton had chosen Senator Albert Gore of Tennessee to run for vice president. Gore was a respected expert on defense and environmental policy. This was a smart move, because voters saw Gore as someone who could handle the presidency should something happen to Clinton.

On the last day of the Democratic convention in July 1992, Perot pulled out of the race because he felt that he and his family were coming under personal attack. Many thought he was a quitter, and it made Clinton look good. Through attacks and scandals, Clinton had kept campaigning.

Bush was nominated at the Republican convention in August. He tried to remind voters of the flaws he saw in Clinton's character, but in October Bush still trailed Clinton by 10 points in the polls.

Then, in a strange twist, Perot said he had "made a mistake" in quitting the race and jumped back in. A few weeks before the election, Clinton, Bush, and Perot had a debate on television. The race seemed close as the election neared.

But on election day it was Clinton who won,

pulling 43 percent of the vote to Bush's 38 percent, while Perot finished a distant third with 19 percent. Clinton won in thirty-two states, and Bush carried the remaining eighteen.

Clinton's victory seemed to mean big changes ahead in America, away from the policies of the Reagan-Bush era. On election night, Clinton saw great things in the nation's future. "With high hopes and brave hearts," he said, standing in front of the Old State House in downtown Little Rock, "the American people have voted to make a new beginning."

On *January 20, 1993,* William J. Clinton was sworn in to office. Candidate Clinton had made many promises. Now it was time for President Clinton to make good on them.

He had promised:

- to boost the country's weak economy.
- to make immediate progress on health-care reform.
- to act on gun control, crime prevention, and increased police protection for citizens.

- to sign NAFTA and GATT, two agreements that he believed would help America's trade relationships with other countries in North America and the world.
- to reform the welfare system.
- to make the government less wasteful.

During President Clinton's first two years in office, progress was made in all these areas. The economy improved, many new laws were signed, and many proposals were developed and presented. But there were also some disappointments and problems, especially with health-care reform. Many Americans had no health insurance; no guarantee they could pay for their own or their families' medical expenses. President Clinton appointed his wife to lead a task force to recommend how the medical-care system in the United States should be changed.

Many people did not think it was proper for President Clinton to appoint his wife to this job. There was also a lot of criticism of the way Hillary Clinton ran the task force. When the report was finished, it was attacked. Still, there was good discussion, and it looked like some positive changes would happen. But at that moment—November 1993—a new scandal made headlines.

"Whitewater" was the name of a land development project in Arkansas. When he had been governor of Arkansas, Clinton and his wife had been involved in the deal with a man named James Mac Dougal and some other people. Mac Dougal was now being accused of stealing money and breaking other laws, and it looked to many as if the Clintons had been involved. Many demanded a full inquiry, but the Democratic majority in Congress called off an investigation.

Vincent Foster, the Clintons' lawyer, had moved to Washington with them, and had an office in the White House. He, too, had been involved in the Whitewater deal, and in July of 1993 he had committed suicide. A file about Whitewater had been removed from his office, and the President and his wife refused to give that file or any other files about Whitewater to the investigators. President Clinton and Mrs. Clinton denied having done or known about anything illegal, but to many they did not seem to be telling the whole truth.

The Whitewater accusations increased and continued into 1994. Also, late in 1993, two men who had worked for Clinton when he was governor told reporters they had helped him to arrange affairs and secret meetings with women in hotel rooms. Another woman, Paula Jones, brought a lawsuit against President Clinton, accusing him of improper advances toward her when he was governor of Arkansas. All these accusations again raised questions about the character of President Clinton. They also distracted the President and his administration from work on health-care reform and other important issues.

The Republicans took advantage of the public's doubts. In the 1994 congressional elections, Republicans won a majority in both the Senate and the House of Representatives—something that had not happened for decades. The next two years of the Clinton presidency looked like they would be his last.

Although under attack, no clear evidence in any of these cases or accusations ever showed that the President or Hillary Clinton had broken any laws. After the midterm elections of 1994, President Clinton continued with his work, much as he had done when dealing with similar problems during the 1992 campaign. There was work to be done to try to secure peace in the Middle East, and President Clinton got the leaders of Israel and Jordan to meet at the White House and begin peace talks. At that meeting in September 1994, Israel and Jordan signed a historic peace agreement.

There was also a war raging in Bosnia. President Clinton and his secretary of state, Warren Christopher, organized a summit meeting. Late in 1995, the three leaders of the warring areas of the former Yugoslavia signed a peace accord in Dayton, Ohio, as a step toward ending the war.

Furthermore, Russia was in a state of turmoil after the collapse of the Soviet Union, and President Clinton worked to support the growth of democracy there. He supported Russia's request for loans to help the economy, and also met with the Russian president, Boris Yeltsin, to be sure that Russia's nuclear weapons would be kept under safe control.

During 1994 and 1995 the Clinton administration's relationship with Congress was strained almost to the breaking point. President Clinton did not want to pass the laws proposed by the Republicans in Congress, and the Republican Congress did not want to advance President Clinton's programs. In particular, neither side would accept the budget proposals of the other. Both sides were so stubborn that for six days in November 1995 the federal government had to shut down because there was no money approved to pay the workers! Disruptions to government services lasted for months. Both sides were responsible, but opinion polls showed that more people believed the Republicans were mostly to blame.

By the beginning of 1996, the nation began to focus on the upcoming presidential election. Bob Dole, U.S. senator from Kansas, was well on his way to becoming the Republican candidate for president. Senator Dole, a World War II veteran, criticized President Clinton for avoiding military service. He criticized him for changing positions on issues, and for not keeping promises made in the 1992 campaign. After Dole became the official candidate, he said that President Clinton had shown that he could not be trusted. He also began to talk about the need for a big tax cut, and accused the Democrats of

In late 1995, the federal government shut down because President Clinton and the Republican Congress could not come to an agreement on the budget. Most government agencies, including the Smithsonian Institution in Washington, D.C., were closed.

MUSEUM HOURS
9:45 a.m. - 5:30 p.m.

Due to the Federal Government shutdown, the Smithsonian Institution must be closed.

We regret the inconvenience.

At the Republican National Convention in San Diego, California, candidate Bob Dole announced that his running mate would be Congressman Jack Kemp from New York.

constantly taking more tax money from American workers.

Opinion polls showed that many people, especially women and younger voters, did not think Bob Dole was a good choice. A lot of people felt that at age 73, he was too old, and perhaps was thinking too much about the past and not enough about the future. Some people thought he would do more for business and wealthy people than he would for families and workers. President Clinton, at age 50, was much younger, and campaigned on the slogan "Building a Bridge to the 21st Century."

As he had been in 1992, Ross Perot was also in the race as the candidate for the Progressive party. Though Perot had little chance of winning, he still wanted to keep important issues in front of the public. He was very angry when he was not allowed to be part of the two presidential debates that were held during the fall of 1996. One of Perot's key issues was campaign-finance reform. He told people that companies and organizations often give huge sums of money to help someone win an election. After that person wins, the organization that donated money may be able to influence decisions.

Optimistic about the outcome of the election, the Clinton family, Hillary (left), Chelsea (center), and Bill celebrated at the Democratic National Convention.

Perot argued that this is not the way a democracy is supposed to work. Perot was not taken very seriously, but in fact, during the last days of the campaign, it was learned that an agent of a foreign country had apparently donated a lot of money to the Democratic party. This looked like an illegal donation, and it added to the questions people had about their choices for president in the 1996 election.

As *election day approached,* opinion polls reflected what voters seemed to be thinking:

"Perot doesn't really have a chance. So the choice is between Clinton and Dole. Dole may be a more honest person, but no one has really proven that Clinton has done anything illegal. The economy is definitely better, and the big tax cut Dole is planning might not be good. I'm not thrilled with President Clinton, but he seems the best choice for now."

Clinton was clearly ahead in the opinion polls as election day arrived.

As predicted, President Clinton was reelected. He won 39 states for a total of 379 electoral votes, and Senator Dole won 19 states, only 159 electoral

Ready to face the challenges of another term as president of the United States, Bill Clinton, with Vice President Al Gore, Gore's wife, Tipper, and Hillary Clinton looking on, makes a speech the day after the 1996 election.

votes. Perot won only 8 percent of the popular vote, far less than he had in 1992.

Although President Clinton won, less than 50 percent of all the people who voted chose him. Also, the Republicans kept control of both the Senate and the House of Representatives, promising a challenging second term for the Clinton administration.

Clinton was the first Democratic president elected to serve a second term since Franklin D. Roosevelt in the 1940s. But just as significant, not since the Great Depression had the Republicans held control of Congress two congressional terms in a row. The American people had left the power in Washington clearly divided.

Standing on the steps of the Old State House in Little Rock, Arkansas, as he had in 1992, Clinton made this statement: "I thank the people of my beloved native state. I would not be anywhere else in the world tonight. In front of this old Capitol that has seen so much of my own life and our state's history, I thank you for staying with me for so long, for never giving up, for always knowing we could do better. . . . My fellow Americans, we have work to do, and that's what this election is all about."

IMPORTANT DATES

August 19, 1946	William Jefferson Blythe IV (Bill Clinton) is born in Hope, Arkansas.
1948	Graduates from Georgetown University, Washington, D.C.
	Attends Oxford University, England, on a Rhodes scholarship.
1973	Graduates from the Yale School of Law, New Haven, Connecticut.
1975	Marries Hillary Rodham.
1976	Elected Arkansas attorney general.
1978	Elected governor of Arkansas.
1980	Loses the governorship to Republican Frank White.
1982	Reelected governor of Arkansas.
1984	Elected for a third term as governor.
1986	Elected for a fourth (four-year) term.
1990	Elected for a fifth term.
October 3, 1991	Announces his candidacy for president of the United States.

July 16, 1992	Accepts the nomination of the Democratic party for the presidency.
November 3, 1992	Wins the election for president of the United States.
February 5, 1993	Signs the Family and Medical Leave Act into law.
September 13, 1993	Witnesses signing of Israeli-Palestinian Declaration of Principles, after which Yitzhak Rabin and Yasir Arafat shake hands at the White House.
Novembr 30, 1993	Signs into law the Brady Bill, which requires a five-day waiting period when purchasing a handgun.
December 8, 1993	Signs NAFTA (North American Free Trade Agreement) into law.
September 13, 1994	Signs a major anti-crime bill into law.
November 21, 1995	Dayton Peace Accord is signed by warring factions from the former Yugoslavia.
November 30, 1995	Visits Belfast, Northern Ireland, to support peace process.
August 20, 1996	Accepts Democratic nomination for reelection.
November 5, 1996	Wins election to a second term as president of the United States.

INDEX

Page numbers in *italics* refer to illustrations.